This edition published in 1998 by
Sebastian Kelly
2 Rectory Road, Oxford, OX4 1BW

© Anness Publishing Limited 1995

Produced by
Anness Publishing Limited
Hermes House
88-89 Blackfriars Road
London SE1 8HA

ISBN 1-84081-019-X

A CIP catalogue record for this book
is available from the British Library

Publisher Joanna Lorenz
Editorial Consultant Jackie Fortey
Senior Editor Belinda Wilkinson

Printed and bound in France

1 3 5 7 9 10 8 6 4 2

A
Storyteller Book

Red Riding
Hood

Retold by Lesley Young
Illustrated by Jenny Williams

Sebastian Kelly

There was once a little girl who lived on the edge of a forest with her mother and father. She loved to play outside among the trees even when it was cold and frosty, so her mother made her a bright red cloak with a hood to keep her warm. But her daughter liked it so much that she wore it all year round, and soon she became known as Red Riding Hood.

One day her mother said to her,

"Your grandmother is ill, so I want you to go and visit her and cheer her up. I have made some cakes and put them in this basket. Stop on the way at the dairy for fresh butter, at the miller's for fresh bread, and at the farmyard for fresh eggs."

Red Riding Hood's mother handed her daughter the basket.

"Now, off you go but remember," she warned, "watch out for wolves. They are crafty creatures and are not to be trusted."

Red Riding Hood put the basket over her arm and set off. She had not gone very far, when a hungry wolf, padding through the forest, stopped and sniffed the air.

"I smell fresh cakes," he said to himself. Then he sniffed the air again.

"Even better," the wolf thought gleefully, "I smell a lovely fresh tasty child."

He slunk silently through the trees until he saw Red Riding Hood's cloak glowing in the distance.

The wolf tucked his tail between his legs, and padded softly over the ground, after her.

Red Riding Hood skipped along until she came to the dairy.

"Hello?" she called out.

There was no answer. Where was the dairymaid?

Red Riding Hood went into the cool milk shed where the cows stood in a row, swishing their tails.

There was still no sign of the dairymaid, so she walked around the back of the dairy into the fresh green field where the cows liked to graze.

"Oh!" gasped Red Riding Hood excitedly when she saw what was there.

A light brown cow was standing beside the dairymaid, and they were both looking down at a tiny, new-born calf.

"How sweet!" said Red Riding Hood.

"Sweet it may be," said the dairymaid, wiping her brow with her freckled arm, "but it was a real surprise. This calf wasn't expected for a couple of weeks – and now it's been born out in the field instead of in a barn with soft straw. I can't leave it here – it's beginning to get cold already – and all the cows are waiting to be milked."

At once, Red Riding Hood took off her cloak and put it over the calf, who looked up at her with huge brown eyes.

"Can you stay here while I run and fetch a wheelbarrow lined with straw?" asked the dairymaid.

When she came back, the dairymaid lifted the calf gently into the barrow and wheeled it off to the barn, its mother following behind, mooing.

Red Riding Hood put her cloak back on, and was about to go on her way, when suddenly she remembered why she had stopped at the dairy.

"The butter!" she cried, "I almost forgot. May I have some fresh
butter for my grandmother, as she's not well?"

"Of course," said the dairymaid, taking a chunk out of a
barrel and shaping it quickly into a block.

"Take this as a thank-you for lending your lovely red cloak.
The calf was just beginning to shiver when you arrived."

Red Riding Hood put the butter in her basket, and skipped
on her way.

The wolf saw her red hood, bobbing up and down in the distance, and zig-zagged quietly through the trees, after her.

Soon Red Riding Hood saw the sails of the mill turning around in the wind up ahead, and she ran up the path.

Usually the miller came out to greet her, but there was no sign of him.

Red Riding Hood pushed open the heavy wooden door, and looked inside. The miller was sitting on a stool, his head in his hands, staring at the white, dusty floor.

"What is the matter?" asked Red Riding Hood.

"You'll never believe this," he answered sadly, shaking his head so that a cloud of flour flew into the air, "but I've run out of sacks. I sent out a big order of flour this morning, and my new sacks haven't arrived yet. That means I can't carry the flour down to the oven and bake a batch of loaves for my special customers – like you."

"It also means," he added glumly, "no bread for my supper."

Red Riding Hood took off her cloak and held it out to him.

"Pile the flour onto my cloak and we'll carry it to the kitchen together."

The miller leaped to his feet and rushed off to the mound of flour which had collected at the bottom of a chute. He scooped it on to the cloak, and he and Red Riding Hood carried it carefully, between them, down to the kitchen.

The oven was hot and ready, so, the miller quickly mixed and kneaded some dough and shaped it into loaves. Then he sprinkled them with flour and put them in the oven.

"Time for a rest and a drink," he smiled, and poured out two glasses of cool lemonade.

Soon a wonderful yeasty smell filled the kitchen. The miller opened the oven, and took out the loaves with his long, flat wooden paddle.

"We'll give your red cloak a good shake outside," said the miller.

"Thank you," said Red Riding Hood. "Oh, and I almost forgot, may I have a loaf of bread for my grandmother. I'm on my way to visit her because she is ill."

"Of course," said the miller, and he chose the largest, flouriest warm loaf and put it in her basket.

"I don't know what I would have done without your red cloak," he said, waving to her at the gate.

Red Riding Hood skipped on her way, and the wolf pricked up his ears as twigs snapped under her feet.

"Ah, there she is, I thought I'd lost her," he said to himself, and he quietly got up and crept after her.

Red Riding Hood ran along until she reached the farmyard. The wolf slunk back when she went through the gate. The farmer had a big gun, and he would love to shoot the wolf, who had eaten many of his chickens in the past.

"Oh no!" growled the wolf. "Missed her again. But I can wait."

Meanwhile, Red Riding Hood looked all round the farmyard. Where was the farmer?

At last she found him, standing at the edge of the duck pond, scratching his head.

"What's the matter?" asked Red Riding Hood.

"It's that silly duck," said the farmer, pointing to the middle of the pond.

"It's got its foot stuck in some weeds, and it can't move. The water is too deep for me to wade out, and I don't know what will happen when it gets dark."

Red Riding Hood looked around the yard until she saw the lid of a large wooden box used for packing eggs. She pushed it onto the water, sat on it, and held out her red cloak like a sail.

The wind caught her cloak, and it ballooned out behind her, sending her speeding across the pond until she reached the duck. She managed to untangle its foot, and it was so tired that it let her lift it on to the lid and sail back to the bank.

"Bless my soul!" said the farmer, helping her onto dry land and taking the duck from her.

He put the duck gently on the ground, and it waddled off, quacking loudly.

"Come inside and have something to eat," said the farmer.

"I can't," said Red Riding Hood, "I'm on my way to visit my grandmother, who's ill."

"And that reminds me, may I have some new-laid eggs for her?" she asked.

"It's the least I can do," said the farmer, and he packed half a dozen large ones among some straw in her basket.

"Thank you. Goodbye!" called Red Riding Hood, and she skipped on her way.

The wolf watched Red Riding Hood leave the farmyard. He came out from his hiding place and raced around ahead of her. Then he sauntered back until he met her coming the other way.

"What a lovely day!" he said, smiling and licking his lips, "And where are you off to, my dear?"

He was so friendly that Red Riding Hood forgot all about her mother's warning to watch out for wolves.

"I'm off to visit my grandmother, who lives in the cottage on the other side of the forest," she answered.

The wolf thought quickly. Perhaps he could manage to have a larger meal than the one he had planned. A two-course one!

"How lucky your grandmother is to have such a pretty visitor," smiled the wolf.

"Does she like visitors?"

"Oh she loves them," said Red Riding Hood, "because she lives all alone."

"Does she really?" said the wolf, showing his large white teeth in a grin,

"Well I'm sure she'll have a lovely surprise. Goodbye and good luck."

The wolf waved his paw.

"Mother was quite wrong," said Red Riding Hood to herself as she skipped on her way, "I think wolves are very charming, handsome animals . . ."

She stopped at a clearing in the middle of the forest to pick some flowers for her grandmother.

"Just one more," she said as she picked each one, running from clump to clump, until a whole hour had passed and she had gathered a huge bunch.

"Grandmother will love these," she thought, and she skipped happily on her way.

The wolf, however, didn't waste any time. He raced between the trees and arrived very quickly at the cottage on the other side of the forest.

He knocked on the door and an old, frail voice called out, "Who's there?"

"It's me, dear Grandmother," replied the wolf in a small high voice.

"Red Riding Hood, who else?"

"I'm in bed, but the door's open, my dear, so just push it and come in."

The wolf pushed open the door and his bright eyes darted round the room until he saw the bed, with Red Riding Hood's grandmother propped up on the pillows, a white lacy nightcap on her head.

The wolf hadn't eaten for two days and his mouth watered. The old woman didn't even have time to scream. He bounded over to the bed and gobbled Grandmother up so quickly that she slipped down his throat before she knew what was happening!

The wolf put on her nightcap and leaped in between the bedcovers, making sure his tail was tucked well out of sight. Then he snuggled down in the warm bed and waited.

Soon there was a knock at the door.

"Who's there?" called the wolf, making his voice sound as
much like the poor old woman he had swallowed as he could.
   "It's me, Grandmother, Red Riding Hood. I've come to cheer
you up, and I've brought you some cakes, some butter, some
new bread and some fresh eggs. Oh – and also a huge bunch of
flowers, because I know how much you love them."

"Not only that, continued Red Riding Hood but I've had lots of adventures on my way here, and I'll tell you all about them."

"That sounds so exciting," croaked the crafty wolf, "come in, my dear."

"I can tell by your voice that you've got a bad cold," said Red Riding Hood, coming into the cottage.

"That's right, my precious," said the wolf hoarsely, "better stay back a bit in case you catch it."

Red Riding Hood looked over to the bed, where the wolf's face was peeping over the edge of the blankets.

"You don't look like yourself at all today, Grandmother," said Red Riding Hood. "I think I got here just in time."

"I think so, too" said the wolf, trying hard not to burp. He had swallowed the old woman so fast that he was suffering from dreadful rumblings and pains in his stomach.

"Grandmother!" said Red Riding Hood, "How big and shiny your eyes seem today!"

"All the better to see you with, dear one," croaked the wolf.

"And how long and pointed your nose looks all of a sudden."

"All the better to smell you with," snarled the wolf softly, licking his lips.

"And your ears," went on Red Riding Hood, "seem to be sticking straight up like antennae."

"All the better to hear you with," smiled the wolf, wiggling them from side to side.

"As for your teeth," said Red Riding Hood, backing away slightly, "they're absolutely enormous!"

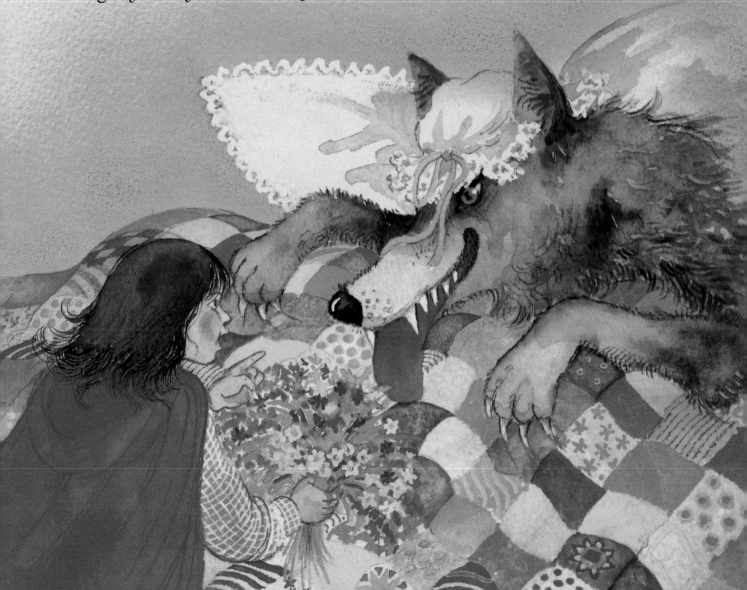

"All the better to eat you with!" roared the wolf, bounding from the bed and swallowing her down in one huge gulp!

After such a large two-course meal, the wolf felt very full and sleepy, so he climbed back into bed and was soon fast asleep and snoring as loudly as a foghorn. A woodcutter was passing by when he was stopped in his tracks by the noise.

"I knew the old woman in that cottage was ill," he said to himself, "but if she's making that much noise, she must be really bad. I'd better drop in and see how she is."

He pushed open the door and saw the wolf, his head lolling against the pillow in its nightcap and his mouth wide open and snoring loudly.

The woodcutter saw at once what had happened. He rushed forward, threw back the bedcovers and before the wolf knew what was happening, the woodcutter had slit open the wolf's stomach with his axe.

Red Riding Hood jumped out, followed by her grandmother, blinking in the light.

"Oh, thank you," she cried, "it was horrible in there and so dark and damp."

The woodcutter filled the wolf's stomach with large stones and the old woman sewed it up with her strongest darning thread.

Then the woodcutter and Red Riding Hood carried the wolf to the lake behind the cottage and threw him in. There were a few bubbles and he sank without trace.

Back inside the cottage, Red Riding Hood's grandmother had a
fire going and was putting some water on to boil.

"I feel so much better," she said, "I think the shock of being
inside the wolf's stomach has cured me. Now, I hope you can
both stay for supper."

"At last," laughed Red Riding Hood, "now I can taste the cakes, the bread, the butter and the eggs, and tell you the story of what happened on my way here."

"I think I've had enough excitement for one day," said her grandmother, spreading butter on some bread.

"Quite right," boomed the woodcutter in his deep voice, stroking the polished axe on his knee.

"When you've eaten, Red Riding Hood, I will take you home through the forest."

"I think you'll find that word of what's happened will spread through the forest as quick as lightning, and you'll never ever again be troubled by a big bad wolf."

And he was right.